Nelle and Alice
The Garden Crawler

Margarete Rougier

2018 by Margarete Rougier

ISBN CreateSpace 12345-678

Back in the garden where Nelle and Alice play;
Lives a furry caterpillar crawling on his way.

His motion like ripple-waves, wobbling through terrain.
No bones in his body, just tell me how, explain!

Nelle and Alice spot him, "Look, there! Can you see?"
Nelle wants to pick him up, Alice says, "Let me!"

Gently resting down her hand, he slowly inches up.
"What a ticklish feeling", in laughter they both erupt.

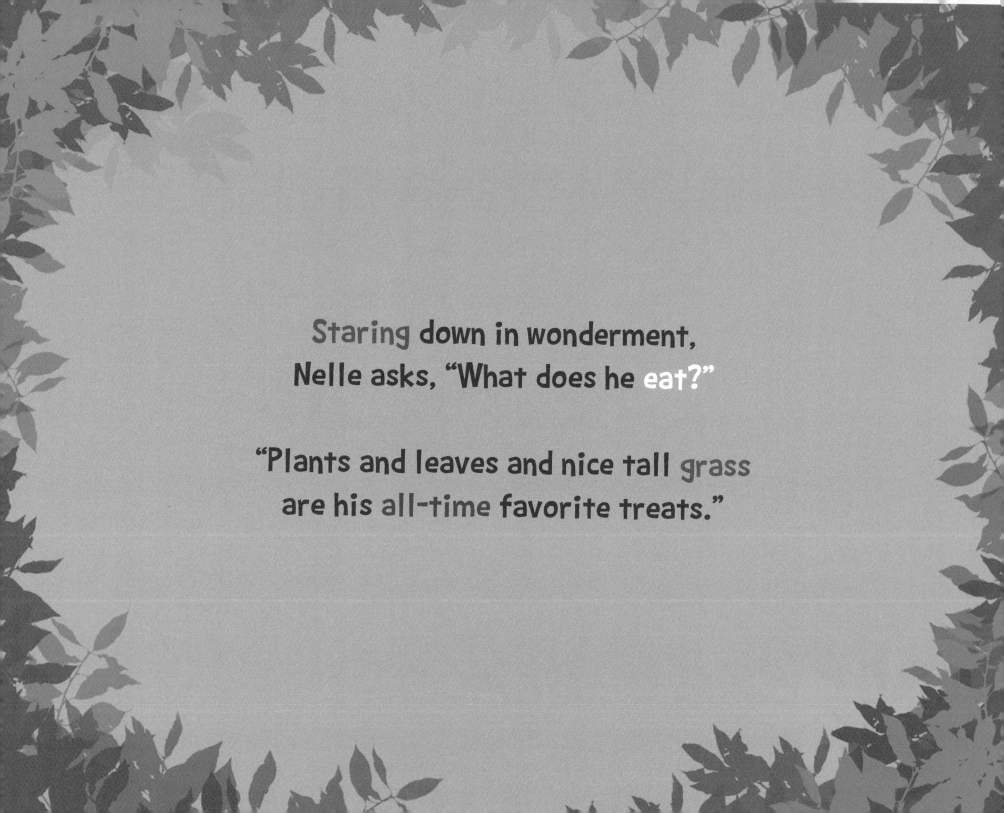

Staring down in wonderment,
Nelle asks, "What does he eat?"

"Plants and leaves and nice tall grass
are his all-time favorite treats."

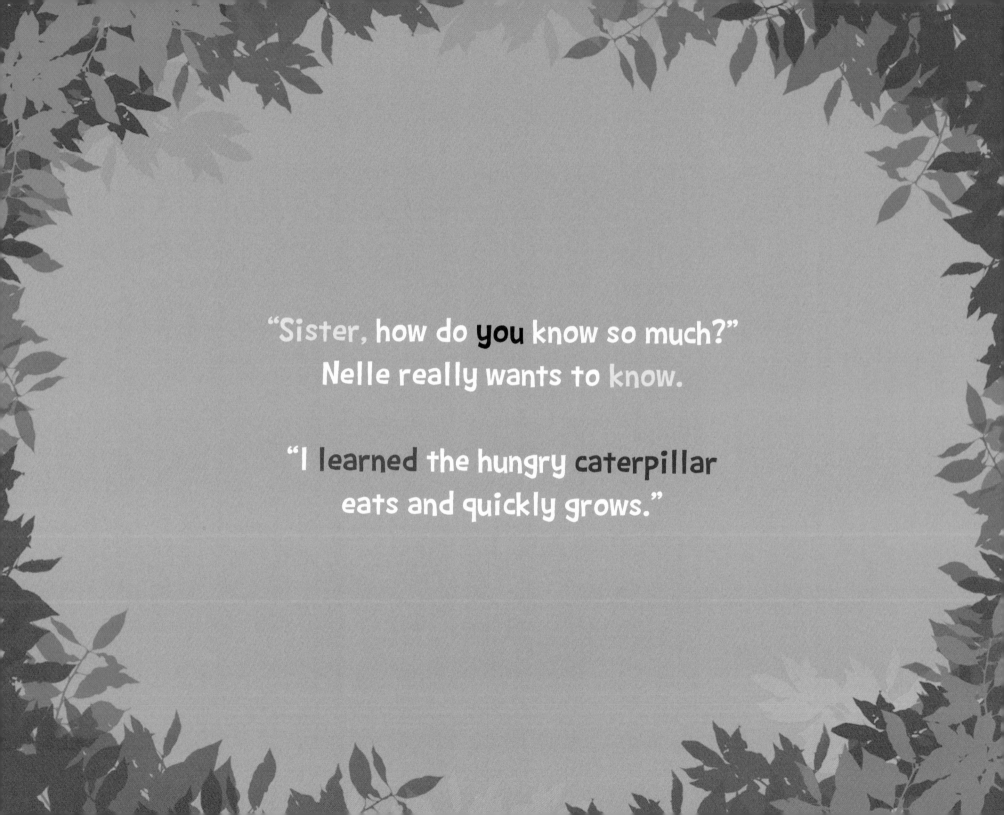

"Sister, how do you know so much?"
Nelle really wants to know.

"I learned the hungry caterpillar
eats and quickly grows."

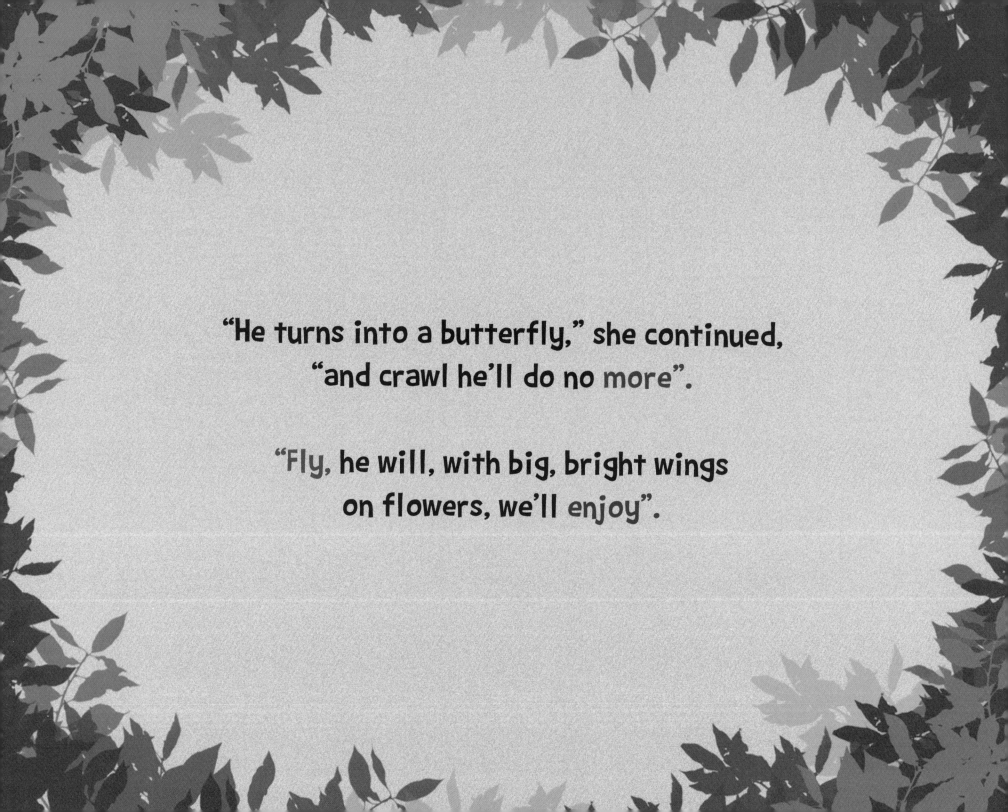

"He turns into a butterfly," she continued,
"and crawl he'll do no more".

"Fly, he will, with big, bright wings
on flowers, we'll enjoy".

It's time now to put him down
and send him on his way.

To explore our garden fresh and green,
the place we like to play.

Careful now, and watch your step,
we want him safe and free.

Let's place him on the zucchini plant
underneath our leafy tree.

Our adventure is now over, it's time to go inside.
We'll tell about our little friend that we had to run and hide.

Nelle and Alice, more awaits you right outside your door.
Waiting for you to discover the world you can explore!

THE END

This book is dedicated to Nelle and Alice,
May you always find wonderment and appreciation in the little things

CPSIA information can be obtained at www.ICGtesting.com
Printed in the USA
BVIW12n0215270918
528601BV00006BA/9